Introducing Pop Monsters...

Deep in the heart of the Pacific Northwest there lives a furry band of critters that come in all shapes and sizes. In that wooded glen, among the misty meadows and mossy-bearded trees, they share fun and adventure in a magical place called Wetmore Forest.

STERLING CHILDREN'S BOOKS
New York

An Imprint of Sterling Publishing Co., Inc.
1166 Avenue of the Americas
New York, NY 10036

ISBN 978-1-4549-3488-2

For information about custom editions, special sales, and premium and corporate purchases, please contact Sterling Special Sales at 800-805-5489 or specialsales@sterlingpublishing.com.

Manufactured in China
Lot #:
2 4 6 8 10 9 7 5 3 1
03/19

sterlingpublishing.com

BUTTERHORN
MAKES SOME FRIENDS

A WETMORE FOREST STORY

By Randy Harvey and Sean Wilkinson
Illustrated by John Skewes

STERLING CHILDREN'S BOOKS
New York

ne day in Wetmore Forest, Butterhorn was in her kitchen cooking when she saw her best friend, Snuggletooth, walking by.

"Hey Snugs," Butterhorn called out. "Where are you off to?"

"Brackenball practice," Snuggletooth said. "Big match coming up."

"Want to come by later for lunch? I just started making some Snodgrass dumplings."

"Yes!" said Snuggletooth. "Snodgrass dumplings will be delicious after a long Brackenball practice. And I can bring some Beetlebark pie for dessert."

"Perfect," said Butterhorn. "A nice quiet lunch."

"Just the two of us,"
Snuggletooth agreed.

Butterhorn **loved** picnics!

She wanted everything to be just right for her
dear friend. She quickly got to work.

Out in the garden, she proudly draped her favorite tablecloth over the stump-top table and set out two place settings. A Fickle-flower made for the perfect centerpiece.

"Well," said Butterhorn good-naturedly. "This just won't do."

Butterhorn tried to cheer
the little flower up. . .

. . .but nothing seemed to work

Butterhorn went into the house and returned a
moment later with a big book and a shiny black stone.
She opened the book and searched through the pages.

"Let's see," she said. "I know it's in here somewhere."

Reading from the book, Butterhorn whispered a secret spell under her breath as she aimed the magic stone at the little flower.

"This ought to do the trick," she said, and the stone began to

GLOW.

Suddenly, a bright beam of light shot out of the stone, sending Butterhorn toppling to the ground.

The beam missed the little flower and hit a small patch of mushrooms at the far end of the garden.

"Hmm," she said. "That's strange. Nothing happened."

"Let's just give that another try. I want everything to be perfect for Snuggletooth!"

Butterhorn tried **again**...

...and **again**...

...and **again**...

...but each time, her aim was just a little off.

A little while later, Snuggletooth arrived at
Butterhorn's house carrying her Beetlebark pie.
She knocked on the door, but no one answered.

Snuggletooth didn't see Butterhorn anywhere.

But she did see some mushrooms walking by.

She decided to follow them.

When Snuggletooth found Butterhorn, she was surrounded by happy, hungry mushrooms. But Butterhorn wasn't happy!

"I'm sorry, Snugs," Butterhorn said, embarrassed. "I guess this isn't the quiet lunch you wanted."

Snuggletooth smiled at her friend. "Don't worry, Butterhorn! What I really cared about was spending time with you."

Butterhorn let out a sigh of relief.

"But I do think we may need some more pie."

Collect all of the

WETMORE FOREST

Adventures.

Available now:

Coming Soon!